Scary Creatures
SWARMS

Written by
Jim Pipe

Created and designed
by David Salariya

Franklin Watts®
An Imprint of Scholastic Inc.
NEW YORK • TORONTO • LONDON • AUCKLAND • SYDNEY
MEXICO CITY • NEW DELHI • HONG KONG
DANBURY, CONNECTICUT

Author:

Jim Pipe studied ancient and modern history at Oxford University and then spent ten years in publishing before becoming a full-time writer. He has written numerous nonfiction books for children, many on history and natural history. He lives in Dublin, Ireland, with his lovely wife, Melissa; and his twin boys, Daniel and Ewan.

Artists:

Janet Baker & Julian Baker
  (JB Illustrations)
John Francis
Carolyn Scrace
Emily Mayer

Series Creator:

David Salariya was born in Dundee, Scotland. In 1989 he established The Salariya Book Company. He has illustrated a wide range of books and has created many new series for publishers in the UK and overseas. He lives in Brighton, England, with his wife, illustrator Shirley Willis, and their son.

Editor: Jamie Pitman

Editorial Assistant:
Rob Walker

Picture Research:
Mark Bergin, Carolyn Franklin

Photo Credits:

t=top, b=bottom

Fotolia: 8, 17t, 25
All other photos istockphoto.com

Yellow crazy ants

Created, designed, and produced by
The Salariya Book Company Ltd
25 Marlborough Place, Brighton BN1 1UB

A CIP catalog record for this title is available from the Library of Congress.

ISBN-13: 978-0-531-21674-3 (lib. bdg.)
978-0-531-21045-1 (pbk.)
ISBN-10: 0-531-21674-8 (lib. bdg.)
0-531-21045-6 (pbk.)

Published in 2010 in the United States by
Franklin Watts
An Imprint of Scholastic Inc.
557 Broadway
New York, NY 10012

Printed in China

PAPER FROM
SUSTAINABLE
FORESTS

Contents

What Is a Swarm?

Swarms are large groups of similar animals such as insects, birds, or fish, all moving in the same direction. Some swarms contain just a few hundred animals, while off the coast of California, billions of shrimp-like **krill** will gather, turning the sea red.

You can see swarms in the air, on the ground, and in the sea. Swarms can appear almost anywhere: from locusts in the desert all the way to mosquitoes in the **Arctic**.

Swarm of locusts

A swarm of bats leaves a cave in Texas.

Huge swarms, such as those created by millions of bats, can appear to move like one big animal. A stream of bats forms huge rings that twist and turn, perhaps to confuse **birds of prey**.

In 1869, giant swarms of ladybugs (also called ladybirds) invaded England. In one city, there were such huge piles of insects in the streets that a new job was created to remove them: "Ladybird shoveler."

Ladybugs swarm together in search of food.

Why Do Animals Swarm?

Animals swarm for many reasons. Fish swim together for protection, since individuals are less likely to be eaten by **predators** when they are in a large group. Ants, termites, and bees swarm to find new homes when the **colony** they are living in gets too crowded.

In the United States, caterpillars called armyworms gobble up all the plants on which they hatch. Then they form large swarms to hunt for food. They strip the leaves from trees, and cover roads and houses.

Which swarms travel the farthest?

Every year, more than 300 million monarch butterflies **migrate** from Canada to Mexico in a massive swarm. Some have even crossed the Pacific Ocean to Australia and New Zealand!

Monarch butterflies

Did You Know?

Swarming can make it easier to find a **mate** in the jungle. In jungles in Thailand, thousands of male fireflies gather in **mangrove** swamps, creating a glowing cloud above the water.

Did You Know?

In Canada, garter snakes swarm together in underground dens. For eight months, they stay rolled up in balls to keep warm. In the spring, they emerge together, like a great wriggling river.

Red-sided garter snakes make dens in **limestone pits**.

Why Are Swarms Scary?

Have you ever walked through a cloud of flies? Imagine meeting a swarm of locusts so thick that it blocks out the Sun!

Groups of stinging animals such as bees can be dangerous, but most swarms are trying to find food or mates—not hurt you.

Did You Know?

Perhaps the scariest swarms of all are groups of red-bellied piranhas on the hunt. The fish's mouths are stuffed with razor-sharp teeth. Luckily, attacks on humans are rare.

Red-bellied piranhas live in the Amazon River basin.

Swarm of locusts in South Africa

Would you like to meet millions of creepy crawlies scuttling across the ground in a giant swarm?

Some people are scared of flying swarms since small insects can easily get into your mouth, go up your nose, or splatter onto your arms.

What's the deadliest swarm?

The Australian box jellyfish is perhaps the deadliest animal that lives in swarms. The sting of a box jellyfish is so poisonous that it can kill a person in just three minutes.

Jellyfish warning sign

What Are the Biggest Swarms?

In 1954, a swarm of five billion desert locusts flew over Kenya. Another swarm was over 1,865 miles (3,000 km) long! However, locusts gather in the desert only when rain creates fresh green shoots. The longer it rains, the larger the swarm becomes. The locusts soon eat everything around them and are forced to go on the move.

Did You Know?

In 1875, a swarm of over three trillion locusts flew down from the Rocky Mountains and gobbled up 50 tons of crops each day on the Great Plains.

Plagues of locusts have been recorded since ancient times.

Which **cannibals** swarm?

Millions of Mormon crickets crawl across western North America in columns up to 5 miles (8 km) long, in search of protein and salt. The crickets have to keep marching fast. If they don't, hungry crickets behind them will eat them.

Female Mormon cricket

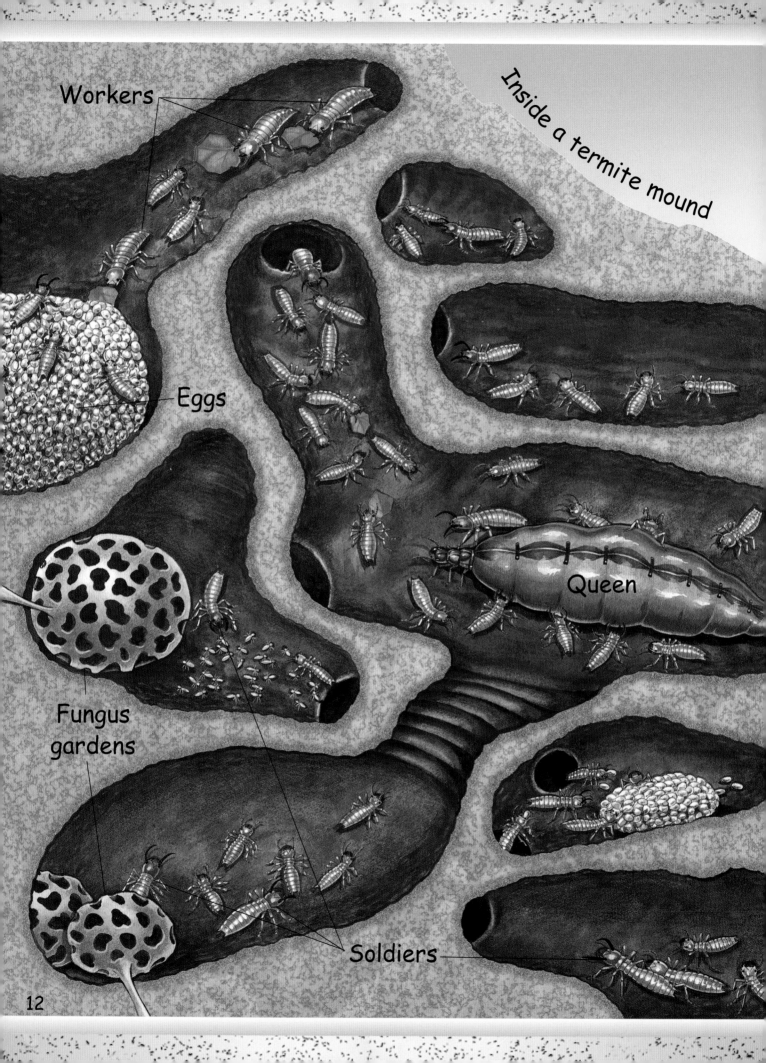

Workers

Eggs

Fungus gardens

Queen

Soldiers

12

What Animals Swarm Along Highways?

Termites swarm to start new colonies. They can build huge mounds with long corridors. These corridors are connected by small openings that can be easily defended by soldier termites if the colony is attacked.

In the rain forests of South America, army ants swarm over the forest floor, eating every small creature in their path. The colony sends out 150,000 blind ants in a column up to 33 feet (10 m) wide, which follow three-lane "highways" laid down by seeing **scouts**. The blind ants return in the middle lane, using their **antennae** to avoid bumping into other ants.

Army ants can kill spiders, scorpions, frogs, and lizards.

Killer bees

Are bees dangerous?

Bee stings may be painful, but for most people they're not dangerous. If someone dies from a bee sting, it is usually because he or she was allergic to the sting. One man was stung 2,000 times and survived. To be safe, stay away from all bee swarms and hives.

What Are Killer Bees?

Bees swarm when their colony gets too crowded. The **queen** leaves the nest with a swarm of **workers**. They cluster together while a few scouts search for a good place for a new nest, such as a hollow tree. If you leave them alone, these swarms won't attack you.

So-called killer bees are aggressive honeybees that were brought from Africa to America by humans. They will chase you for more than half a mile if you get too close to their hive!

Did You Know?

Honeybees are very useful to humans. They help **pollinate** flowers and provide us with honey and wax.

14

A swarm of bees the size of a tennis ball contains about 3,000 bees, while a swarm the size of a basketball contains over 50,000.

Only honeybees swarm—wasps and bumblebees do not. Yellowjackets, however, will gather in great numbers to attack to protect their nest.

Yellowjacket wasp

Bees swarming to form a new hive.

What Is the Loudest Swarm?

The mating call of the cicada is so noisy that it can drown out lawn mowers and telephones. If you had been in Indiana in May 2004, you might have seen billions of cicada **nymphs** climb out of the soil and march up the nearest tree or pole.

After they hatch, the cicada nymphs burrow underground, where they feed for 13 or 17 years before returning to the surface. Then they turn into adults, mate, and lay eggs—all in just a few weeks.

Did You Know?

Predators such as chipmunks and birds feed on cicadas until they can't eat any more. Birds may become too full to fly!

Cicada

Cicadas provide a feast for birds, snakes, moles, and wasps. Cicadas don't bite or sting, but they survive through sheer numbers. More than a trillion can appear in just a few nights.

Like many cockroaches, the Madagascar hissing cockroach may swarm, but it also makes a great pet! It lives up to its name by forcing air through holes in its body to produce a hissing sound when it is threatened or when it is fighting.

Madagascar hissing cockroaches

Male frogs croak in a chorus to attract females. The tiny painted reed frog has the loudest frog call for its size. Male frogs can be heard almost 1.25 miles (2 km) away from their pond.

Did You Know?

In the countries of Malaysia, Burma, and China, grilled cicadas are a delicious (and nutritious) snack. Females are usually tastier because they have more meat on them!

Croaking frogs

Why Do Birds Flock Together?

Birds flock together for food or safety. Starlings, blackbirds, and pigeons all form huge **flocks** that wheel around in the sky or look for food on the ground. Gulls gather in big numbers on **mudflats** to feed.

Other birds nest together in huge colonies for safety. Having many eyes together makes sure that some birds will spot predators while others are feeding, snoozing, or just looking the other way.

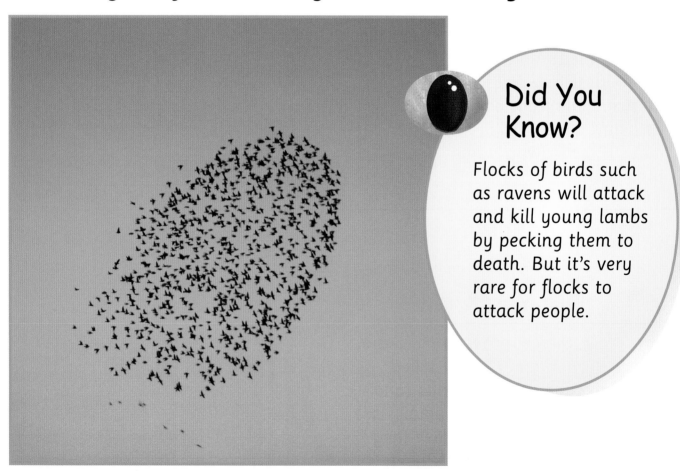

Flock of starlings

Did You Know?

Flocks of birds such as ravens will attack and kill young lambs by pecking them to death. But it's very rare for flocks to attack people.

Flocks of snow geese

Some birds flock together to go on long migrations. Snow geese fly in flocks of 100 to 1,000 that are made up of many family groups.

The geese can fly for up to 70 straight hours, traveling 1,680 miles (2,700 km) from the Arctic to the Gulf of Mexico. They fly in a "V" shape. This saves energy because the birds in the back can coast in the **slipstream** made by the birds in front of them.

Colony of northern gannets

Big colonies provide protection for sea birds, which are clumsy on land.

Bass Rock, off the eastern coast of Scotland, is home to 150,000 gannets. From a distance the island looks white because there are so many birds nesting on it.

What Animals Swarm in a School?

Fish can swim together in large groups known as **schools**, usually with other fish of a similar size and **species**. Most swim together for protection. A large school twisting and turning can look like a bigger animal, and this confuses predators.

A school is a tight group of fish moving as one. A **shoal** is a loose group of fish swimming together socially, rather than to protect against predators.

X-Ray Vision

Hold the next page up to the light and see why this school of fish is in danger.

See what happens

Did You Know?

Goldfish can find food more quickly in a big school. Swimming together may also help fish to save energy by swimming in the slipstream of fish in front of them.

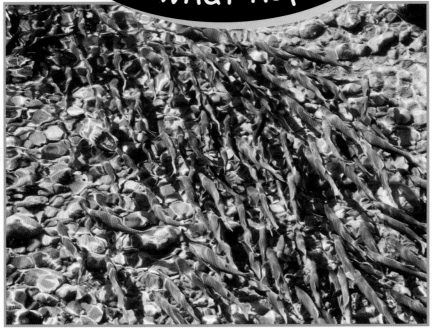

Spawning salmon

Pacific salmon live most of their lives in the ocean, but as adults they return to the streams where they hatched in order to lay their eggs.

Some migrate over 2,000 miles (3,200 km) and then swim upstream, fighting **rapids** and leaping over waterfalls. They gather in huge numbers, **spawn**, and then die.

Sardines

Gannets

Herring gull

Shark

Dolphin

What Is a Bait Ball?

When attacked, some shoals of fish pack tightly together to form a school. Some schools do sudden U-turns or "explode" as the fish swim in all directions.

A **bait ball** occurs when sharks or dolphins herd a shoal of sardines toward the surface and force them into a tight ball. Birds can spot the trapped sardines from the air. Sharks, dolphins, and gannets all go into a **feeding frenzy**, gobbling up the sardines.

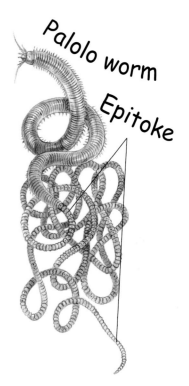

Palolo worm

Epitoke

What worm swarms?

The palolo worm spends most of the year living in the coral of the Caribbean Sea, feeding off life forms in the coral.

Then, when the conditions and climate are just right, the worm's rear end, called the epitoke, breaks off and becomes a separate animal! This swims to the surface and breeds in swarms.

Fish forming a defensive ball

Do Lemmings Really Try to Kill Themselves?

Not really, no. Lemmings are small **rodents**, usually found in the Arctic. They have long, soft fur and very short tails. Lemmings spend most of their time on their own, meeting other lemmings only to breed.

However, every four years, the Norway lemmings breed so fast that they are forced to migrate in enormous numbers. If a large group gets stuck in a small valley, they panic and flee in all directions. Some even swim across water. It is not yet known why this breeding frenzy occurs so regularly.

Norway lemmings

Some people think that groups of lemmings purposely jump off cliffs. But lemmings don't try to kill themselves. What actually happens is that some are forced off cliffs when there are too many of them there.

Others drown when they are pushed into the sea as more and more lemmings arrive at the shore.

Other rodents live together in large numbers. According to the legend of the Pied Piper, the German town of Hamelin had a plague of rats in 1284. Today many towns and cities have a similar problem.

In Mizoram, India, the government pays local people to kill the hordes of rats that thrive on bamboo that grows in the area. In Paris, there are four rats to every human.

Did You Know?

In the summer of 2007, northwestern Spain was crawling with more than seven million voles. These furry rodents munched their way through wheat and potato crops.

In some Indian temples, swarms of rats are sacred.

Do Big Animals Swarm?

It's not just small animals that swarm—some grazing animals live and travel together in big numbers. In North America, giant herds of more than 120,000 caribou travel over 3,100 miles (5,000 km) each year. The lands they live on in summer become windy and harsh in the winter. So as cold weather approaches, they move to a place where it is warmer and there is more food.

Every year, 200,000 zebras and 400,000 Thomson's gazelles join 1.5 million wildebeests on a journey across the African plains. They travel in search of food and water, crossing sun-baked plains and crocodile-infested rivers.

By keeping on the move, they stay one step ahead of predators such as lions and leopards.

Long-beaked common dolphins

Do sharks swarm?

Yes! Several hundred adult lemon sharks swarm off the coast of Jupiter, Florida, each year to find mates. Schools of up to 500 hammerhead sharks gather to mate in the Gulf of California.

Hundreds of dolphins have also been known to gather in a school to feed together.

A caribou herd crossing a river

Did You Know?

Up to 500 white beluga whales travel in groups called pods. During the breeding season, thousands of belugas meet together in river mouths and mate.

Can Humans Cause Swarms?

Humans accidentally introduced yellow crazy ants to Christmas Island, Australia, about 80 years ago. Soon the ants started to swarm. Now super-colonies of these ants threaten the 100 million red crabs that leave the island's forest and crawl to the sea to breed every year.

In 1859, a farmer brought 24 rabbits to Australia. Within just a few years, millions of rabbits had spread across southern Australia, partly because they had no predators. Since then, by eating plants and destroying habitats, the rabbits have wiped out local species and put others in danger.

Red crabs crossing a road on Christmas Island, Australia.

Jellyfish in the sea off the coast of Norway

Yellow crazy ants get their name from their jerky, erratic movements. They live in nests of over 35,000 workers. They kill their **prey**—spiders, **mollusks**, and crabs—by spraying them with acid from their bodies.

Yellow crazy ants

Can pollution create swarms?

The polluted waters near big coastal cities such as Tokyo, Sydney, and Miami are attracting trillions of jellyfish. With no natural predators, swarms of them are hunting in packs and wiping out large shoals of fish.

Did You Know?

Global warming is also creating more insect swarms. In January 2007 a dry, warm winter led to a locust invasion in the Yucatán Peninsula in Mexico.

Swarm Facts

A locust swarm can quickly eat farmers out of house and home. In 1957, a single locust swarm destroyed nearly 187,400 tons (170,000 metric tons) of grain in Somalia—enough to feed a million people for a year.

Flying swarms are often at the mercy of the winds. Over 100 years ago, a huge locust swarm in South Africa was blown out to sea. After tides swept the dead insects to shore, they formed a wall that was 4 feet (1.2 m) deep and stretched for 50 miles (80 km) along the coast.

Columns of army ants can travel at speeds of up to 66 feet (20 m) per hour and may contain 20 million ants.

Swarms of yellow crazy ants have killed over 20 million red crabs on Christmas Island in recent years.

Fire ants are red, black, or yellow ants with a sting that burns like fire. They travel in swarms and can invade people's homes. They may also attack the young of ground-nesting birds.

Cicadas come out of the ground in **broods**. Some broods appear every 17 years, others every 13 years. The biggest group, known as Brood X, will next appear in 2021.

In 2004, scientists glued tiny transmitters onto the backs of Mormon crickets to track their movements. They found that crickets who strayed from the main swarm were much more likely to be eaten by birds and other predators.

The weight of all the termites in Africa is greater than the combined weight of all the zebras, wildebeests, elephants, and other grazing animals. That's a lot of termites!

In November 2007, a 9.3-mile (15-km) wide, 43-foot (13-m) deep swarm of mauve stinger jellyfish wiped out Northern Ireland's only salmon farm. The surrounding sea turned red with all the jellyfish.

Red-bellied piranhas hunt in groups of about 20 to 30 fish. Like sharks, they are highly attracted to the scent of blood. The group of piranhas scatter to look for prey. When potential food is found, the scout uses sound to send a message to the others. This works because piranhas can hear very well.

Glossary

antennae Feelers on each side of an insect's head.

Arctic The icy region around Earth's North Pole.

bait ball A group of fish forced to the water's surface by sharks or dolphins.

birds of prey Birds that make especially good predators.

brood A group of young, all born at the same time.

cannibal A creature that eats one of its own species.

colony A group of animals living together. When several colonies of the same animal work together, they form a super-colony.

feeding frenzy When animals react to a large number of prey by eating as fast as they can.

flock A group of birds flying or feeding together.

global warming The gradual increase of Earth's temperature.

krill Small, shrimp-like crustaceans that swim in huge swarms.

limestone pit A quarry or canyon made of limestone.

mangrove A tree that grows on wet, salty land.

mate A partner of the same species that an animal can reproduce with.

migrate To take a long journey to another habitat due to predators or weather conditions.

mollusk An animal with a soft body (and sometimes a shell), such as snails, clams, slugs, squid, and octopuses.

mudflat A muddy coastal area that forms when mud is deposited by the tides.

nymph A young form of an insect that changes into an adult by repeatedly shedding its skin.

plague A huge number of animals that devastates a habitat.

pollinate To transfer pollen from one plant to another.

predator An animal that kills and eats other animals.

prey An animal that is hunted by other animals.

queen The only female that can breed in a colony of ants, bees, or termites.

rapid A steep part of a river where the water flows very fast.

rodent A mammal, such as a mouse or rat, that has large teeth in its upper and lower jaws for gnawing food.

school A tight group of fish from the same species that moves and acts as one.

scout An animal that checks the area ahead for food or predators.

shoal A loose group of fish from the same species.

slipstream In this book: an effect caused when animals push air or water out of their way, making it easier for animals behind them to gain speed.

spawn To lay eggs in water.

species A group of animals or plants that look the same, live in the same way, and produce young that do the same.

swarm A large group of animals moving in the same direction.

worker An ant, bee, or termite that cannot breed but finds food and cares for the queen and her young.

Index